COLOR CHAOS!

Lynn Rowe Reed

Holiday House

New York

To my editor,
Mary Cash,
who is always
complimentary
of my work

Library of Congress Cataloging-in-Publication Data
Reed, Lynn Rowe.
Color Chaos / by Lynn Rowe Reed. — 1st ed.
p. cm.
Summary: When substitute principal Mr. Greystone prohibits colors at Hughes Elementary School,
it takes a visit from illustrator Maurice Coleur to set things right. Includes information about primary,
secondary, and tertiary colors and the color wheel.
ISBN 978-0-8234-2257-9 (hardcover)
[1. Color—Fiction. 2. Schools—Fiction. 3. Illustrators—Fiction.] I. Title.
PZ7.R25273Day 2010   [E] —dc22   2009029053

The text typeface is Gill Sans Bold.
The artwork was created with acrylic paint, colored
paper, photographs, and a little bit of Photoshop magic.

One day I made an announcement.

My mother bought me a big box of crayons. I put them in my backpack and dashed off to school.

Just inside the school I met our new substitute principal, Mr. Greystone.

His no's went on and on.

NO RUNNING! NO SHOUTING! NO HOPPING! NO SINGING!

In my classroom, Mrs. Peters wrote the schedule on the board.

I saw that I would have to wait a very long time to use my new crayons.

8:30 Pledge
8:35 math
9:15 social studies
9:45 reading
10:20 language arts
10:45 testing
11:45 lunch
12:15 recess
12:45 spelling bee
1:20 science
2:00 art
2:30 special guest
3:00 dismissal

At lunchtime, I smuggled my crayons into the cafeteria. Next to the lunch line was Mr. Greystone's new board.

We tried out Marvelous Magenta and Dandelion Yellow and Periwinkle Blue and sixty-one other colors.

When Mr. Greystone came in, he blew his stack!

Art supplies in all colors were collected for disposal; recess was canceled. We got extra spelling words.

RULES

NO TALKING
NO SINGING
NO HOPPING
NO SKIPPING
NO WHISTLING
NO HORSEPLAY
NO RUNNING
NO JUMPING
NO GUM CHEWING
NO JOKING
NO FUN...
PERIOD

THERE WILL BE NO MORE CRAYONS...
NO MORE MARKERS...
NO MORE COLOR OF ANY KIND...
AT HUGHES ELEMENTARY!

Meanwhile . . .

inside the trash can

CRAYONS 48

CRAYONS 16

CRAYONS 64

CRAYONS 24

It's awfully black in this trash can.
What's wrong with that?
Let's stay calm.
ORANGE
BLACK
BLUE

While the crayons argued, Maurice Coleur, the famous illustrator of *Purple Eggs and Jam*, was arriving.

As we gathered in the cafeteria for his presentation, we were all too excited to notice that something was missing.

Back in the trash can, the confiscated crayons were still bickering.

You guys are all nuts!
We should be working together
to find a way out of here!

Here?
Is this where I belong?
YELLOW
ORANGE
Would primary colors Yellow, Red, and Blue step forward? Next I will position the secondary colors Green, Orange, and myself. The rest of you—in the tertiary family—should find all the right places to slip into.
RED
I think I'll take a nap.
RED PURPLE

VOILÀ! The colors all found their proper places on the color wheel but needed a way out of the trash can.

Try as they might, there was no wiggling the lid from the can.

All this time, Mr. Coleur continued his presentation.
At the end of his talk, he took questions.

Mr. Coleur reached
into his portfolio
and pulled out
a handful
of illustrations.

YIKES! What has happened to my beautiful colors? Where are my brightly hued paintings?

PURPLE EGGS AND

Mr. Coleur was so upset that he fainted, hitting his head against the trash can on his descent.

JUMPING JELLY BEANS!
I SEE COLOR, AND IT IS EVERYWHERE!

We held our breath
while Mr. Greystone
helped Maurice Coleur
to his feet.

Would our
principal
flip his lid?

MR. COLEUR'S LESSON

Making a color wheel is simple.
Draw a large circle.
Color the **primary** colors first:
yellow, red, and blue.
A primary color is a color from which
all other colors are made.

Then add the **secondary** colors:
orange, purple, and green.

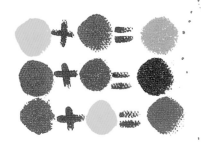

A secondary color is a
color you make by mixing
two primary colors.

The **tertiary** colors come next.
A tertiary color is made by mixing a
primary color with a secondary color.
Some tertiary colors are
yellow orange, red purple, and blue green.

ON COLOR

What is a complementary color?

My, Red, don't you look beautiful today?

You are so-o-o-o-o complimentary, Green.

A color's complementary is the color directly opposite it on the color wheel. Red, for example, is the complement of green.

ANALOGOUS COLORS are any three colors that are side by side on the color wheel.

Yes, love thy neighbor.

It's a good thing we get along.

HUE is the name of a color.

TINT is a color plus white.

Shade is a color plus black.

WARM COLORS
SUN
HOT AS THE
COOL COLORS
COOL AS A
cucumber
VALUE
VALUE is the lightness or darkness of a hue.

POP QUIZ

QUESTIONS:

(1) What color was Mr. Greystone seeing when his board was ruined?

(2) What color was Mr. Coleur feeling when he said good-bye to the kids at the end of the day?

(3) What color has the illustrator of this book painted her toenails?

(4) What is the color of the building one block south of the publishing house that published this book?

(5) What would be a good title for this book?

COLOR CHAOS!

ANSWERS:

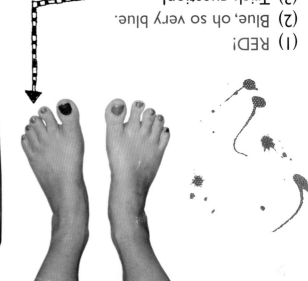

(1) RED!

(2) Blue, oh so very blue.

(3) Trick question!

(4) Another trick question! You would have to take a trip to New York to find the correct building and answer!

(5) MR. GREYSTONE'S LONG, LONG NO'S
A GREY DAY AT HU(GH)ES ELEMENTARY
SNOT = YELLOW + BLUE (Actually, there's no snot in this book at all, but the author believes kids think snot is a funny word.)
THIS BOOK NEEDS A TITLE! (This is such a catchy title that I think I'll save it for later.)